The

CAT NEXT DOOR

Story and Pictures

by

Elizabeth Koda-Callan

WORKMAN PUBLISHING, NEW YORK

Library of Congress Cataloging-in-Publication Data

Koda-Callan, Elizabeth.
The cat next door/written and illustrated by Elizabeth Koda-Callan.
p. cm.
Summary: A young girl cares for her neighbor's cat and learns responsibility so that she can have a kitten of her own. Includes tiny silver cat charm on a silver chain tucked inside the cover.

ISBN 1-56305-502-3
[1. Pet cats — Fiction. 2. Self-confidence — Fiction.] I. Title
PZ7.K8175Cat 1993
[E] — dc20   93-2219
                                                         CIP
                                                         AC

Workman books are available at special discounts when purchased in bulk for premiums and sales promotions, as well as for fundraising or educational use. Special editions can also be created to specification. For details, contact the Special Sales Director at the address below.

Workman Publishing Company, Inc.
708 Broadway
New York, New York 10003
Printed in Hong Kong
First printing November 1993
10 9 8 7 6 5 4 3

For Ellen Rongstad and Alex Mallen
and
Cinnamon, Clover, Doc,
Mona, Max, Eddie, Jazzbow,
Mabel, Ozzie, and Winnie

Once there was a little girl who wanted a pet. Not just any pet, but one that would snuggle under her chin and purr in her ear. She wanted a kitten.

But when she asked her mother for a kitten, her mother said, "Do you remember who fed the hamster you brought home from school?"

The little girl looked down at her shoes. "Well, you did, but . . . "

"And who cleaned the gerbil's cage?"

"You did . . . but . . . if I had a kitten of my own . . ."

Her mother shook her head. "I don't think you're ready to have a kitten," she said. "Taking care of an animal is a big responsibility."

The little girl sighed.

A few days later a neighbor came to visit. "I have to go away tomorrow," she said, "but I haven't been able to find anyone to take care of my cat, Clover."

"Oh, I'd love to come over and play with her," said the little girl eagerly.

"I'll be gone for a whole week," the neighbor said. "You would have to do more than play with her. You'd have to feed her, and give her fresh water, and clean her litter box every day."

"I can do it," said the little girl. "I know I can!"

She looked at her mother. Her mother looked at the neighbor. "Oh, may I? Please?" the little girl asked.

"Well," said her mother, "I suppose it's all right if you think you can do it."

"Great," said the neighbor. "Come and I'll show you where I keep Clover's food, her dishes, and her litter box."

When they went next door, the neighbor's cat ran to her and rubbed against her leg. Clover was a silver tabby with dark gray stripes, small white paws, and a dash of white on the tip of her tail.

"She's so beautiful," thought the little girl. She couldn't wait to begin taking care of her.

But her first day with the silver tabby wasn't easy. When the little girl entered the kitchen, she could see the cat watching her from behind a chair. Clover wouldn't come out until there was food in her dish and water in her saucer. The little girl found out quickly that cats don't always come when you call them.

The little girl also found out that she had to wait while Clover ate slowly and carefully. And when she drank, she took the longest time to lap water with her little pink tongue.

The second day when the little girl arrived, the cat was waiting to be fed. But Clover never purred, and she didn't want to be petted.

"You have to be patient," the little girl's mother said. "Give her time to get to know you."

And that's just what the little girl did.

One day the little girl had an idea.
She crumpled a piece of paper into a ball
and tied it with a long piece of string.

She slowly dragged the paper across the
floor. A few seconds later a streak of silver
fur pounced on the paper toy.

Then she tossed the paper in the air
and the silver tabby leaped up and batted

it with her paw. The cat and the little
girl played for nearly an hour.

The following day when the little girl walked into the kitchen, Clover came to greet her. She even meowed a welcome.

Then something more unexpected happened. As the little girl went to get the cat food, she felt soft fur rub against her leg. She reached down to pet the silver tabby for the very first time. The little girl smiled and the cat purred. By the end of the week Clover began to trust the little girl more and more and the little girl began to understand what the cat needed.

When the neighbor returned from her trip, she was pleased to see that her silver tabby seemed well fed and content.

"You've done a wonderful job," the neighbor told the little girl, and she handed her a small white box tied with a red ribbon.

When the little girl opened the box, she saw a necklace resting on blue velvet. It was a sparkling silver tabby on a silver chain.

"This necklace will remind you of how well you took care of my silver tabby," said the neighbor.

"I'm going to miss her," said the little girl as she put on the necklace.

"Well, you may come and visit her whenever you like. I can see you've become good friends."

The little girl thanked the neighbor and ran home to show her mother the necklace.

"Look," she said. "It's a silver tabby, just like Clover."

"It's lovely," said her mother. "I'm proud of you for doing such a good job."

That evening the little girl thought that even though it was fun to have the neighbor's cat for a friend, it wasn't the same as having her very own kitten.

Several weeks later, the neighbor stopped by to invite the little girl and her mother for a visit.

"I made a new toy for Clover," said the little girl. "Shall I bring it?"

"I'm afraid Clover won't be able to play today," the neighbor said.

The little girl was disappointed. "Why not?" she asked.

"Something very special has happened. Come and see."

The little girl bounded into the kitchen ahead of her mother and the neighbor, calling to the cat. There was no answering meow.

"Where is she?" asked the little girl.

The neighbor smiled. "Follow me."

She led them to the guest room, where the shades were drawn. The room was dark and quiet, but then the little girl heard tiny squeaking sounds. There in the corner she saw the neighbor's silver tabby lying on a pillow, surrounded by four furry little bodies.

"Kittens!" cried the little girl. "Clover has kittens!"

Yes," said the neighbor. "Four fine kittens. Which one would you like?"

The little girl looked up at her mother, wide-eyed.

"May I have one?"

Her mother smiled and nodded.

"Which one? They're all so cute," said the little girl. Then she saw a striped kitten that looked just like the neighbor's cat.

"This one. The little silver tabby." she said. "May I take her home now?"

"Not yet," the neighbor answered. "But soon."

"How soon?" the little girl asked.

"As soon as the kitten is ready to leave its mother."

So the little girl had to be content to visit her kitten every day. But it was so hard to wait!

At last, one morning, the neighbor called and asked, "Would you like to take your kitten home today?"

"Oh, yes," said the little girl.

She proudly carried her new kitten home in a small box she had lined with a soft cloth.

At home, the little girl looked down at her necklace and her new silver tabby. She stroked the kitten's soft silver fur, and she held the little tabby under her chin.

"Now I have the kitten I've always wanted," she thought. "And what's even better, I know I can take care of her."

The silver tabby purred in her ear, and gently batted the silver necklace with one tiny white paw.

About the Author

Elizabeth Koda-Callan is a designer, illustrator, and best-selling children's book author. She lives in New York City with her cat, Cinnamon, a very independent orange tabby.

She is the creator of the Magic Charm book series, which includes THE MAGIC LOCKET, THE SILVER SLIPPERS, THE GOOD LUCK PONY, THE TINY ANGEL, and THE SHINY SKATES.